Merry Christmas 1997
To Eric and Emlyn

From Uncle John Schalow

HEIAN INTERNATIONAL, INC.
1815 W. 205th Street, Suite 301
Torrance, CA 90501

First American Edition 1996
00 99 98 97 96 10 9 8 7 6 5 4 3 2 1

Translated by Dianne Ooka
Edited by Monique Leahey Sugimoto

ISBN: 0-89346-837-1

Printed in Hong Kong

BEST-LOVED CHILDREN'S SONGS FROM JAPAN

These songs are to be sung in Japanese for which the transliteration is provided.

SOMEWHERE SPRING

Somewhere...somewhere...spring is on its way,
Somewhere...somewhere...a stream is starting to flow again.

Somewhere...somewhere...a lark is singing excitedly,
Somewhere...somewhere...buds are bursting forth.

The cold east winds of March still blow,
But somewhere...somewhere...spring is on its way.

どこかで春が

作詞　百田宗治
作曲　草川　信

どこかで「春」が
生まれてる
どこかで水が
ながれ出す

どこかでひばりが
ないている
どこかで芽の出る
音がする

山の三月
東風吹いて
どこかで「春」が
生まれてる

MY SECRET

Shu! Hey, Mom...I have a secret...
    A secret...a secret...
Mom, you're always smiling...
    Let me whisper it in your ear!

Shu! Hey, Mom...I have a secret...
    A secret wish...a secret wish...
Mom, tomorrow is Sunday, isn't it...isn't it?
    Please listen to my wish!

Shu! Hey, Mom...I have a secret...
    A secret...a secret...
Mom, I want to spend the day with you and only you...
    Just the two of us...all day long!

ないしょ話

作詞　結城よしを
作曲　山口保治

一　ないしょ　ないしょ
　　ないしょの話は　あのねのね
　　にこにこ　にっこり　ね　母ちゃん
　　お耳へ　こっそり　あのねのね
　　坊やのおねがい　きいてよね

二　ないしょ　ないしょ
　　ないしょのおねがい　あのねのね
　　あしたの日曜ね　母ちゃん
　　ほんとにいいでしょ　あのねのね
　　坊やのおねがい　きいてよね

三　ないしょ　ないしょ
　　ないしょの話は　あのねのね
　　お耳へ　こっそり　ね　母ちゃん
　　知っているのは　あのねのね
　　坊やと母ちゃん　二人だけ

4

NA I SHO NA I SHO NA I SHO NO HA NA SHI WA A NO NE NO NE NI KO NI KO NI KO RI NE KA A

CHAN O MI MI E KO SO RI A NO NE NO NE BO YA NO O NE GA I KI I TE YO NE

SOAP BUBBLES

Soap bubbles floating upward,
      slowly making their way to the roof...
Up they go then...Pop!
      they burst and disappear.

Some bubbles burst,
      before they get to float...
They're made then...Poof!
      they're suddenly gone.

Oh, wind! Please don't blow!
Let our bubbles drift higher and higher up into the sky.

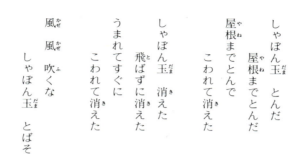

しゃぼん玉

作詞　野口雨情
作曲　中山晋平

しゃぼん玉　とんだ
屋根までとんだ
屋根までとんで
こわれて消えた

しゃぼん玉　消えた
飛ばずに消えた
うまれてすぐに
こわれて消えた

風　風　吹くな
しゃぼん玉　とばそ

SHA BON DA MA　TO N DA　YA NE MA DE　TO N DA　YA NE MA DE　TO N DE　KO WA RE TE　KI E TA　KA ZE KA ZE　FU KU NA　SHA BON DA MA　TO BA SO

THE CANARY

Oh, canary, canary, who's forgotten his song...
> Shall we abandon him in the mountains out back?
> No, no, that won't do...

Oh, canary, canary, who's forgotten his song...
> Shall we bury him in the bamboo thicket?
> No, no, we can't do that either...

Oh, canary, canary, who's forgotten his song...
> Shall we beat him with a willow switch?
> No, no, that would be too cruel...

Take this canary who's forgotten his song,
And put him in an ivory boat with silver oars.
If he's set afloat on a moonlit sea,
He'll soon remember his song!

かなりや

唄を忘れたかなりやは　後ろの山にすてましよか
いえ　いえ　それはなりませぬ

唄を忘れたかなりやは　背戸の小やぶに埋めましよか
いえ　いえ　それもなりませぬ

唄を忘れたかなりやは　柳のむちでぶちましよか
いえ　いえ　それはかわいそう

唄を忘れたかなりやは
象牙の船に　銀の櫂
月夜の海に浮かべれば
忘れた唄をおもいだす

作詞　西條八十
作曲　成田為三

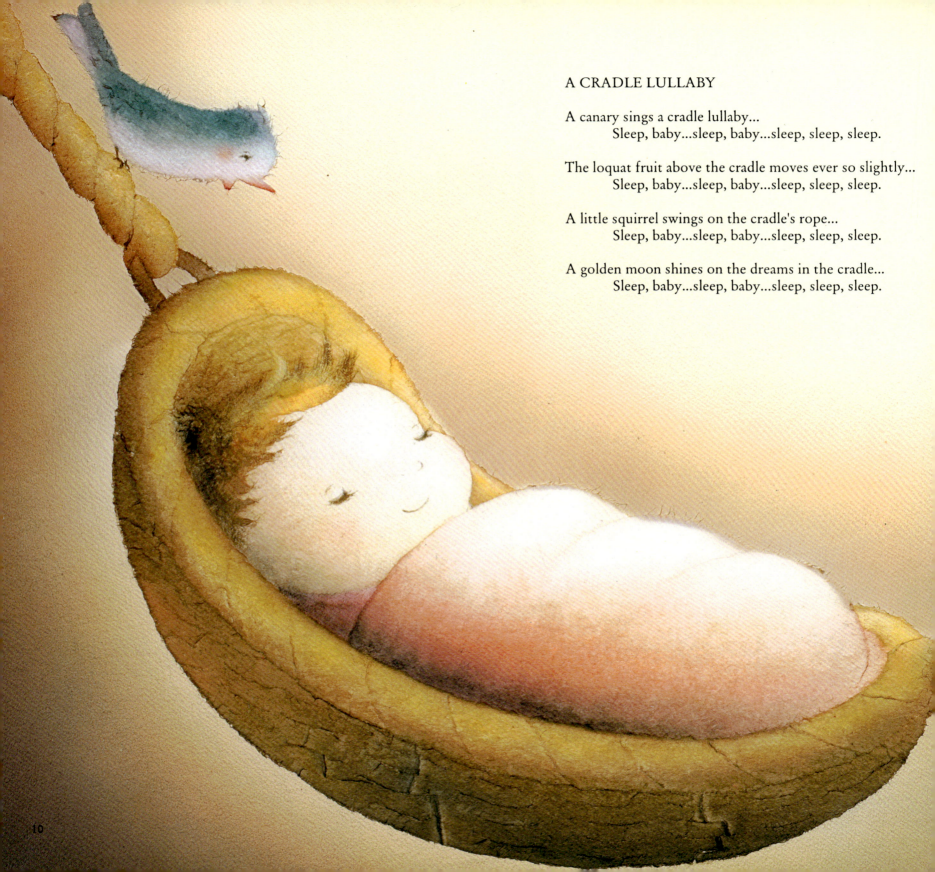

A CRADLE LULLABY

A canary sings a cradle lullaby...
      Sleep, baby...sleep, baby...sleep, sleep, sleep.

The loquat fruit above the cradle moves ever so slightly...
      Sleep, baby...sleep, baby...sleep, sleep, sleep.

A little squirrel swings on the cradle's rope...
      Sleep, baby...sleep, baby...sleep, sleep, sleep.

A golden moon shines on the dreams in the cradle...
      Sleep, baby...sleep, baby...sleep, sleep, sleep.

ゆりかごのうた

作詞　北原白秋

作曲　草川信

一　ゆりかごのうたを
　　カナリヤが歌う よ
　　ねんねこ　ねんねこ
　　ねんねこ　よ

二　ゆりかごのうえに
　　枇杷の実がゆれる よ
　　ねんねこ　ねんねこ
　　ねんねこ　よ

三　ゆりかごのつなを
　　木ねずみがゆする よ
　　ねんねこ　ねんねこ
　　ねんねこ　よ

四　ゆりかごのゆめに
　　黄色い月がかかる よ
　　ねんねこ　ねんねこ
　　ねんねこ　よ

YU RI KA GO NO　U TA O　KA NA RI YA GA　U TA U YO　NE N NE KO－　NE N NE KO　NE N NE KO　YO

LITTLE AUTUMN

Someone...someone has found...
      A little autumn...a little autumn...a little autumn.
Like the blindfolded "It" in Blind Man's Bluff,
      Listening for the hand-clapping players...
I faintly hear the flute-like cry of the wild shrike...
      I've found a little autumn...a little autumn today.

Someone...someone has found...
      A little autumn...a little autumn...a little autumn.
The windows of my room...my room which faces north...
      Are cloudy, like milky vacant eyes.
A crisp autumn gust whistles through the tiny cracks...
      I've found a little autumn...a little autumn today.

Someone...someone has found...
      A little autumn...a little autumn...a little autumn.
The crest of the old weathercock is faded,
      And on it rests a single sumac leaf...
A flaming red sumac leaf the color of the setting sun.
      I've found a little autumn...a little autumn today.

ちいさい秋みつけた

作詞　サトウハチロー
作曲　中田喜直

一　だれかさんが　だれかさんが
　　だれかさんが　みつけた
　　ちいさい秋　ちいさい秋
　　ちいさい秋　みつけた
　　目かくし鬼さん　手のなるほうへ
　　すましたお耳に　かすかにしみた
　　よんでる口笛　もずの声
　　ちいさい秋　ちいさい秋
　　ちいさい秋　みつけた

二　だれかさんが　だれかさんが
　　だれかさんが　みつけた
　　ちいさい秋　ちいさい秋
　　ちいさい秋　みつけた
　　おへやは北むき　くもりのガラス
　　うつろな目の色　とかしたミルク
　　わずかなすきから　秋の風
　　ちいさい秋　ちいさい秋
　　ちいさい秋　みつけた

三　だれかさんが　だれかさんが
　　だれかさんが　みつけた
　　ちいさい秋　ちいさい秋
　　ちいさい秋　みつけた
　　むかしの　むかしの　風見の鳥の
　　ぼやけたとさかに　はぜの葉ひとつ
　　はぜの葉赤くて　入り日色
　　ちいさい秋　ちいさい秋
　　ちいさい秋　みつけた

13

七つの子

作詞　野口雨情
作曲　本居長世

からす　なぜなく
からすは山に
かわい七つの
子があるからよ

かわい　かわいと
からすはなくの
かわいかわいと
なくんだよ

山の古巣へ
いって見てごらん
丸い目をした
いい子だよ

SEVEN BABIES

Why does the crow caw?
She caws because she has seven cute chicks back in her mountain nest.

"Caw! Caw!" goes the crow.
"I love you! I love you!" she's telling them.

Go to her mountain next...
There you'll see her seven wide-eyed sweet chicks.

KA RA — SU   NA ZE NA KU NO   KA RA SU WA YA MA   NI   KA WA I I   NA NA—TSU NO   KO GA A RU KA RA   YO

KA WA I   KA WA I TO   KA RA SU WA   NA KU NO   KA WA I   KA WA I TO   NA KU N DA   YO

YA MA — NO   FU — RU SU E   I TE MI TE GO RA   N   MA — RU I   ME WO—SHI TA I I—KO DA   YO—

16

RED DRAGONFLY

Oh, red dragonfly...red dragonfly at twilight...
I saw you for the first time while still a baby being carried on my sister's back...
     Could it be that long ago?

Picking mulberries from the mountain field...
And our little baskets...
     Was that all a dream?

My sister got married when she was fifteen...
And moved far, far away.
     She no longer sends news to our village.

Oh, red dragonfly...red dragonfly at twilight...
     I see you resting there on the tip of the bamboo reed.

あかとんぼ

作詞　三木露風
作曲　山田耕筰

一　夕やけ小やけの
　　あかとんぼ
　　負われて見たのは
　　いつの日か

二　山の畑の
　　桑の実を
　　小籠に摘んだは
　　まぼろしか

三　十五でねえやは
　　嫁に行き
　　お里のたよりも
　　絶えはてた

四　夕やけ小やけの
　　あかとんぼ
　　とまっているよ
　　竿の先

YU- YA KE KO YA KE- NO A KA TO N BO　OWA RE TE MI TA NO- WA-　I TSU NO- HI- KA

17

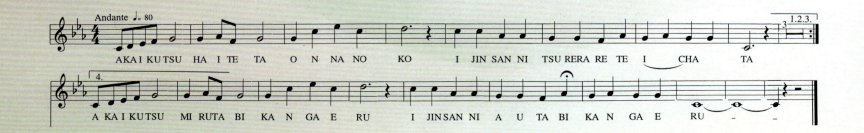

Andante ♩ = 80

AKA I KU TSU HA I TE TA   O N NA NO   KO   I JIN SAN NI   TSU RERA RE TE I   CHA   TA

A KA I KU TSU MI RUTA BI KA N GA E   RU   I JIN SAN NI   A U TA BI KA N GA E   RU

18

RED SHOES

The girl wearing red shoes
      Was taken away...far away.

She boarded a ship at Yokohama Harbor
      And was taken far away.

Her eyes must be blue now,
      Living for so long in that foreign land.

I think of her whenever I see red shoes...
I think of her whenever I see a foreigner...

赤い靴

作詞 野口雨情
作曲 本居長世

赤い靴　はいてた
女の子
異人さんに　つれられて
行っちゃった

横浜の　埠頭から
船にのって
異人さんに　つれられて
行っちゃった

いまでは　青い目に
なっちゃって
異人さんのお国に
いるんだろう

赤い靴　見るたび
かんがえる
異人さんにあうたび
かんがえる

19

THE BLUE-EYED DOLL

The plastic blue-eyed doll from America...
How she cried when she arrived in Japan.

"I don't undestand the language...
Whatever will I do if I get lost...?"

Sweet little Japanese girl...play with her...
Make her feel at home.

青い眼の人形

作詞 野口雨晴
作曲 本居長世

青い眼をした
お人形は
アメリカ生まれの
セルロイド

日本の港へ
ついたとき
いっぱい涙を
うかべてた

「わたしは言葉が
わからない
迷子になったら
なんとしよう」

やさしい日本の
嬢ちゃんよ
仲よく遊んで
やっとくれ
仲よく遊んで
やっとくれ

21

森の小人

作詞　山川　清
作曲　山本雅之

一
森の木かげで　ドンジャラホイ
シャンシャン手びょうし　足びょうし
たいこたたいて　笛ふいて
今夜はお祭り　夢の国
小人さんがそろって　にぎやかに
ア　ホーイホーイヨ　ドンジャラホイ

二
おつむふりふり　ドンジャラホイ
かわいいおててで　踊りだす
三角帽子に　赤い靴
お月さんにこにこ　森の中
小人さんがそろって　おもしろく
ア　ホーイホーイヨ　ドンジャラホイ

三
おててつないで　ドンジャラホイ
ピョンピョンはねはね　輪になって
森の広場を　まわります
今夜は明るい　月の夜
小人さんがそろって　元気よく
ア　ホーイホーイヨ　ドンジャラホイ

四
みんなたのしく　ドンジャラホイ
チョンチョンおててを　打ちあって
夢のお国の　森の中
そろいのお服で　踊ります
小人さんがそろって　楽しそに
ア　ホーイホーイヨ　ドンジャラホイ

LITTLE PEOPLE OF THE FOREST

From the shade of the forest trees...
Clapping hands and stomping feet, all in rhythm with the drums and flutes...
Tonight here's a festival in the land of dreams!
        The little people are all together, singing merrily
        "Hey, hey, ho, ho, hey, ho, ho!"

Shaking their heads and waving their hands...
They begin to dance.
Their pointed caps and flaming red shoes...
How the moon lights up the forest!
        The little people are joyous tonight, singing
        "Hey, hey, ho, ho, hey, ho, ho!"

Joining hands and forming a big circle...
They skip and hop together.
Around and around the forest clearing they go...
Tonight is bright, moonlit night!
        The little people are in high spirits, singing
        "Hey, hey, ho, ho, hey, ho, ho!"

Everybody is happy...
Clapping their hands...they all come together.
Here in the forest in the land of dreams...
They dance and dance in their colorful matching outfits!
        The little people are gathered together, singing cheerfully
        "Hey, hey, ho, ho, hey, ho, ho!"

FOX CUBS

In the mountains, fox cubs play their dress-up game...
Crushed wildflowers color their cheeks
And fallen maple leaves adorn their hair.

In winter, the fox cubs can't play dress-up games...
The withered leaves are too dry to make a suit
And the pretty flowers have long since gone.

The cubs can't play any games back in their den...
Their tails are too fluffy now and just get in the way.
And so they wait restlessly...thinking about the coming spring.

こぎつね

作詞　勝　承夫
ドイツ曲

一　こぎつね　コンコン　山の中　山の中
　　草の実　つぶして　おけしょうしたり
　　もみじの　かんざし　つげのくし

二　こぎつね　コンコン　冬の山　冬の山
　　枯れ葉の着物じゃ　ぬうにもぬえず
　　きれいな　もようの　花もなし

三　こぎつね　コンコン　穴の中　穴の中
　　大きなしっぽは　じゃまにはなるし
　　小首を　かしげて　かんがえる

24

♩=100 mf 2/4

KO GI TSU NE KON KON   YA MA NO NA KA   YA MA NO NA KA   KU SA NO MI

TSU BU SHI TE   O KE SHO   SHI TA RI   MO MI JI NO   KA N ZA SHI TSU GE NO KU   SHI

KA KI NE NO KA KI NE NO MA GA RI KA DO TA KI BI DA TA KI BI DA O CHI BA TA KI

A TA RO KA A TA RO YO KI TA KA ZE PI I PŪ FU I TE I RU

26

たきび

作詞　巽　聖歌
作曲　渡辺　茂

一　かきねの　かきねの　まがりかど
　　たきびだ　たきびだ　おちばたき
　　「あたろうか」「あたろうよ」
　　きたかぜぴいぷう　ふいている

二　さざんか　さざんか　さいたみち
　　たきびだ　たきびだ　おちばたき
　　「あたろうか」「あたろうよ」
　　しもやけおててが　もう　かゆい

三　こがらし　こがらし　さむいみち
　　たきびだ　たきびだ　おちばたき
　　「あたろうか」「あたろうよ」
　　そうだんしながら　あるいてく

THE BONFIRE

It's a bonfire! A big bonfire!
A bonfire of fallen leaves at the corner of the hedge.
"Do you want to get warmed up by the fire?" "Yes! Let's go!"
The cold north wind is blowing hard.

It's a bonfire! A big bonfire!
A bonfire of fallen leaves right where the camellias once bloomed.
"Do you want to get warmed up by the fire?" "Yes! Let's go!"
Their frostbitten hands are already starting to tingle.

It's a bonfire! A big bonfire!
A bonfire of fallen leaves right where the cold wind blows.
"Do you want to get warmed up by the fire?" "Yes! Let's go!"
They walk along toward the fire.

SCOLDED

Scolded...scolded...
Sent to town on an errand...carrying a baby on her back...
She returns late at night...
And on the lonely village outskirts...
She fears the cry of the fox.

Scolded...scolded...
Her eyes fill with tears...but she doesn't cry out...
Their home is on the other side of the mountain...
A village full of flowers...
When will she see its cherry blossoms again?

しかられて

作詞　清水かつら
作曲　弘田竜太郎

しかられて
しかられて
あの子は町まで　おつかいに
この子は坊やを　ねんねしな
夕べさみしい　村はずれ
こんときつねが　なきゃせぬか

しかられて
しかられて
口には出さねど　目になみだ
二人のお里は　あの山を
こえてあなたの　花のむら
ほんに花見は　いつのこと

SHI KA RA RE TE SHI KA RA RE — TE A NO KOWA MACHI MA DE OTSUKAI — NI KO NO KO WA —BŌ — YA O
NEN·NESHI NA YŪ U BE SA MI SHI I MU RA HA ZU RE KON TO KI TSU NE GA — NA KI YA SE NU KA — —

SCOLDED

Scolded...scolded...
Sent to town on an errand...carrying a baby on her back...
She returns late at night...
　　And on the lonely village outskirts...
　　She fears the cry of the fox.

Scolded...scolded...
Her eyes fill with tears...but she doesn't cry out...
Their home is on the other side of the mountain...
　　A village full of flowers...
　　When will she see its cherry blossoms again?

しかられて

作詞　清水かつら
作曲　弘田竜太郎

しかられて
しかられて
あの子は町まで　おつかいに
この子は坊やを　ねんねしな
夕べさみしい　村はずれ
こんときつねが　なきゃせぬか

しかられて
しかられて
口には出さねど　目になみだ
二人のお里は　あの山を
こえてあなたの　花のむら
ほんに花見は　いつのこと

SNOW!

It's snowing! Just look at it coming down!
It falls and falls and keeps piling up.
The mountains and fields are wearing a cottony white cap...
And the bare trees are all at once in bloom again.

It's snowing! Just look at it coming down!
It falls and falls and it seems like it will never stop.
The puppy is excited and running through the newly fallen snow...
And the kitten is curled into a ball, sleeping next to the heater.

雪(ゆき)

文部省唱歌

一　雪やこんこあられやこんこ
　　ふってはふってはずんずんつもる
　　山(やま)も野原(のはら)も綿帽子(わたぼうし)かぶり
　　枯(か)れ木(き)のこらず花(はな)が咲(さ)く

二　雪やこんこあられやこんこ
　　ふってもふってもまだふりやまぬ
　　犬(いぬ)は喜(よろこ)び庭(にわ)かけまわり
　　猫(ねこ)はこたつで丸(まる)くなる

YU - KI YA KON KO   A RA RE YA KON KO   FU TE WA FU TE WA ZU N ZUN TSU MO RU

YA - MA MO NO WA RA MO   WA TA BO SHI KA BU RI   KA RE KI NO KO RA ZU HA NA GA SA KU

31

ABOUT THE SONGS...

SOMEWHERE SPRING
Spring is a season that is always looked forward to in Japan. It marks the end of a usually cold and long winter, and the start of a season of growth and renewal. The blooming of the cherry trees in particular announce the arrival of spring. Many events and activities, such as the start of the school year, are scheduled so that they coincide with the arrival of spring. This song is a celebration of spring. It was published in 1923.

MY SECRET
Traditionally, the raising of children in Japan has been considered the responsibility of the mother. Since children spend a great deal of their preschool years at home with their mothers, children tend to have a strong and close relationship with them. This song captures the peaceful moments between a mother and her child. Yoshi Yuki wrote this song in 1939.

SOAP BUBBLES
The toys children played with in 1939 -- the time this song was written -- were very different from the toys children play with today. Blowing bubbles, playing cards and spinning wooden tops were common forms of play for children at this time.

THE CANARY
Canaries were first brought to Japan in the late 1700s. They were kept as pets because of the beautiful way they sing. This song tells of a canary that has forgotten how to sing and tries to offer ways in which to get the canary to sing its beautiful song again. "The Canary" appeared in 1918 in a magazine which triggered a movement in the art world at that time. It is thought that this song captures the essence of the Taisho Era, the period in Japan just after the introduction of western culture.

A CRADLE LULLABY
Loquat fruit resembles a plum in size and can be either yellow or light orange in color. The fruit usually comes out in summer and is rather sweet. Perhaps the baby in this song is sleeping in a cradle hung on the branches of the loquat tree in the early evening. The "o" sound that ends each Japanese verse expresses the tenderness and softness of a lullaby. Though the song was written in 1921, the freshness of the song can still be felt today.

LITTLE AUTUMN
Just as spring brings the blooming of cherry blossoms, autumn in Japan also has its distinctive characteristics. During the autumn, the leaves of the trees change colors and through the season, one can see a variety of colors from brilliant yellows and reds to rich browns. The game of Blind Man's Bluff is played by blindfolding a player and having him or her located the other players. The blindfolded "It" must listen carefully for the clapping noises made by the other players to try to capture them. This song was first played in 1955 for an autumn festival. It became very popular in the years following its introduction. When sung, it is particularly beautiful accompanied by a piano.

SEVEN BABIES
The cawing sound made by a crow and the word for "cute" are very similar in Japanese. This song plays on this similarity and gives an explanation for the seemingly annoying cawing sound of a crow. Perhaps this song expresses a parent's feeling towards a child who has left home and is living far away. This song was introduced in 1921.

RED DRAGONFLY
Red dragonflies were once a common sight in Japan. They were usually seen at sunset and signaled the end of summer and the beginning of autumn. In this song, Rofu, whose mother died when he was only seven years old, sings about his childhood memories and a nostalgia for the past. This song is perhaps one of the most widely-known songs in Japan. It is so popular that at schools in the author's hometown of Tatsunoshi, the song is played both before and after the school day.

RED SHOES
Yokohama Harbor was one of the first ports open to foreign ships in Japan, and consequently it became a place where many foreigners lived. The city of Yokohama was regarded at that time as a "foreigner town," and considered cosmopolitan and chic. Though it is not clear under what conditions the young girl left Japan, one feels the sorrow caused by her disappearance. "Red Shoes" became so popular that there is a statue of a girl wearing red shoes in Yokohama today. The song made its debut in 1921.

THE BLUE-EYED DOLL
Dolls from America were something of a curiosity when they were first seen in Japan. The shape, size and type of material used to make the dolls were very different than those of the Japanese dolls. The dolls were a visible example of the cultural differences between the United States and Japan. As a gesture of goodwill, the American government once sent American-made dolls to Japan. "The Blue-Eyed Doll" was published in 1921.

LITTLE PEOPLE OF THE FOREST
This is a remake of a popular poem entitled, "Tonight is The Festival on Palau Island/The Natives Gather..." The "little people" of this song were thought to be very cute making this a popular song throughout Japan. It was first sung in 1947.

FOX CUBS
This song is based on a well-known German folk song. Like "Somewhere Spring," it too celebrates the changing of the seasons. The fox cubs can play with the fallen leaves of autumn, but as the weather becomes colder and they are no longer able to play outdoors, they must stay indoors and wait until spring arrives again. This song became widely used in a music textbook for third graders after 1947.

THE BONFIRE
Bonfires were once a common sight throughout Japan, especially right at the end of autumn. In fact, bonfires are still commonly used today in the countryside, to get rid of the fallen autumn leaves. Having a bonfire is usually a communal activity and often after the leaves are burned, yams are roasted in the embers of the fire, making a tasty treat on cold days. The song was first played in 1941.

SCOLDED
In Japan, it was once common for girls to be placed in domestic service and separated from their families. As part of their duties, these young girls had to tend to their masters' children and were even held responsible if the child cried. To avoid being scolded, the girls would go to the outskirts of the town or far enough away so that the crying child could not be heard. There are many stories in Japan about foxes. Foxes are known to have mysterious powers that enable them to bewitch people and so are usually feared. Lonely and afraid of encountering a fox, the young girl in this song tries to comfort herself by thinking of the beautiful flowers in her village. This song first appeared in 1920.

SNOW!
"Snow!" was written in 1911 and is a children's nursery rhyme. The heaters used in Japan in 1911 were probably charcoal heaters. Containers of burning charcoal were placed in an area of the floor especially designed for heating. So that the heat could not escape, a blanket and table top were placed over the container. One got warm by putting the hands and feet under the blanket. The first line of each Japanese verse is interesting; it can be interpreted as either the imitation of the sound of falling snow or as a phrase announcing the falling of the snow itself.